WARNING!
Contains some
Monkey Pirate swearing
and book fairy rudeness!

Have you read this one?

THE MONKEY PIRATES

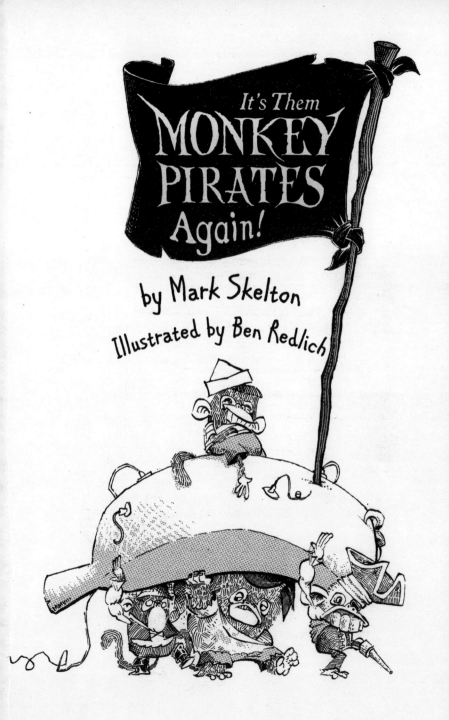

It's Them
MONKEY
PIRATES
Again!

by Mark Skelton

Illustrated by Ben Redlich

EGMONT

We bring stories to life

It's Them Monkey Pirates Again first published 2009
by Egmont UK Limited,
239 Kensington High Street London W8 6SA

Text copyright © 2009 Mark Skelton
Illustrations copyright © 2009 Ben Redlich

The moral rights of the author and illustrator have been asserted

ISBN 978 1 4052 4394 0

1 3 5 7 9 10 8 6 4 2

www.egmont.co.uk

A CIP catalogue record for this title is available
from the British Library

Printed and bound in Great Britain by the CPI Group

CONTENTS

A SHANTY TO START

What shall we do with dem Monkey Pirates?

What shall we do with dem Monkey Pirates?

What shall we do with dem Monkey Pirates?

Travelling to the future!

Way-hey, up they rises,

Way-hey, up they rises,

Way-hey, up they rises,

With bananas in their bellies!

SOMETHING YOU SHOULD KNOW ABOUT THIS BOOK

Like all books, this one has a book fairy and this fairy is about the size of a lengthwise. That is to say, the size of the word 'lengthwise' when placed on the page, like this: ⟶

The fairy for this book goes by the name of Bernard Bumboil and she is a girl. She is invisible, which is just as well because she is particularly dirty.

L
E
N
G
T
H
W
I
S
E

1

However, if you want to see something very interesting, then try this. Say the fairy's name out loud three times, like this: 'Bernard Bumboil! Bernard Bumboil! Bernard Bumboil!'

If you have done this properly you will notice something. If you now look around at the other people in the room, they will all be giving you very strange looks. I suggest that you don't do that again.

The other interesting thing about Bernard Bumboil the fairy is that she likes to rearrange

the words on the page when you close it to make rude ones. In the first book about the Monkey Pirates, for instance, she would make the words 'poo' and 'bum' when the book was closed. Then she would quickly rearrange them back into the story whenever you opened it again. (That's the reason nobody knew about her in the first book.)

Book fairies are impossible to catch out – it's a bit like trying to see if the light goes off when you close the fridge door. Although less cold.

In this book, Bernard Bumboil will be

rearranging the words into even ruder words, words that I can't mention here. So be warned!

Another thing you need to be warned about is her rather nasty habit of leaving little presents and droppings that look like punctuation marks on the page.

So try not to get any question marks (?), asterisks (*), speech marks (' '), commas (,) or indeed exclamation marks (!) on your hands!!!

(Always keep a tissue handy.)

AARRGH!

1

IN WHICH BALDERDASH TRIES TO REMEMBER

'Bless my cotton socks!!' is the sort of thing you might say to yourself if you found twelve monkeys in your wardrobe one night.

'Stone the crows!!' is something else you might utter if you also discovered that these monkeys were dressed as pirates and were

using your wardrobe as their ship to travel through space and time. And 'Polish my old boots with a prize-winning cucumber and call me Susan' if you then discovered that these pirate-dressed monkeys held the clue to the

mysterious disappearance of your beloved Uncle Bartholomew.

However, Emily Jane, who was a very unusual girl, said none of these things when she first met the Monkey Pirates.

They arrived in
her bedroom in
the village of
Linoleum-on-
the-Naze one
windy September

evening, saying 'Aaarrgh!' a lot. Emily Jane
then simply said, 'What are your names and
can I join you?' She felt sure that they could
help her find her Uncle Bartholomew, who
she hadn't seen for ages. He vanished one
day while varnishing a wardrobe. He was an

inventor and he said he'd invented the wardrobe, the banana, the shoe, vinegar-flavoured toothpaste and time travel. He had an enormous beard the size of a small English village and a humphilated laugh, and she missed him. Emily Jane had lost a few things in her time, such as a colourful marble (it was down the back of a sofa) and her sense of direction (it was at the back of a drawer) but she had never lost an entire relative before.

That first Monkey Pirates visit seemed like many moons ago but in fact it was three moons

and forty-five minutes ago.

Emily Jane had learnt many new things –
such as how much Monkey Pirates loved
bananas (you can get a Monkey Pirate to do
pretty much anything for half a banana) and
how a man they called 'the Professor' (and
apparently not her Uncle Bartholomew) had
invented the wardrobe. She had also learnt
how uncomfortable it was sharing any
wardrobe with twelve monkeys.

There were, of course, some things she still didn't know, like why isn't there mouse-flavoured cat food? Why does your nose run and your feet smell? What colour does a chameleon go if you put it on a mirror? And if you were travelling at the speed of light and switched on a torch, what would happen?

So, like most people, Emily Jane knew some things but not everything. Unlike most people though, she did have a fantastically active imagination. An imagination that could be active at the drop of a hat. But not just the

11

drop of any hat. It would have to be a huge Mexican hat the size of a dustbin lid with two moles sitting in it at a table playing a card game that they had invented called 'Don't Tweak My Pig, Clarence Spud'.

See, I told you.

Another thing that Emily Jane had was a gift from one of the Monkey Pirates. She had been given something very special by Balderdash, and it was a time-telescope. The

time-telescope was a thing of ingenious cleverness and it allowed the viewer to see scenes from the past and the future (although Emily Jane wasn't always sure which one she was looking at).

Emily Jane's life had never been the same since the Monkey Pirates had visited her.

And from then on she was always prepared. (She always kept some bananas and her time-telescope close to hand.)

One afternoon, there had been strange noises

coming from Emily Jane's wardrobe, starting with a scratching noise like a mouse in a box, changing to a rattle and then finally a whooping sound. Emily Jane knew that the Monkey Pirates would soon make an appearance. She couldn't wait to see them again!

The door bulged before bursting open.

'Hello there! How have you all been?' asked Emily Jane eagerly as the monkeys tumbled out. (They still hadn't mastered a dignified entrance, she noted.)

The Captain and his crew of Banana

Buccaneers were not expecting to see Emily Jane, but then their destinations were a constant surprise to them. The Monkey Pirates didn't really understand wardrobes, time travel or bananas but they did enjoy them all immensely.

'Bananas and barnacles!' said the Captain, which Emily Jane took as meaning on this particular occasion, 'Fine and thank you for asking.'

And all the Monkey Pirates sat down quietly and thought about their adventures . . . NO,

OF COURSE THEY DIDN'T!!! They picked their noses, scratched and farted, so don't go running off to Jamaica with the idea they didn't!!

In fact, Tosh found something interesting up his nose that he decided to put in his pocket for later.

Balderdash, the fattest of all the Monkey Pirates, looked slightly confused.

'You remember me, don't you?' asked Emily Jane. 'It's me – Emily Jane. You gave me the time-telescope. It is a thing of ingenious

17

cleverness.' She waved it at him.

'Aaaargh! . . . Umm! . . . Aaaaargh!'
Balderdash thought hard. He wasn't sure, but
then his memory was terrible and did often
play tricks on him.

Eventually, after much thinking, he
remembered Emily Jane. She smiled at him
and Balderdash smiled his very special smile
back at her. A smile with many gaps and few
teeth.

Emily Jane was excited to see her pirate
friends again. She said hello to Poppycock,

18

and he smiled at her too. Now, Poppycock's teeth were false and made entirely out of wood. In fact, he had a wooden leg, a hook for a hand, false teeth and a tin ear. (So he should be regarded as a potential fire risk.) But he was also a great Monkey Pirate. He stood on his one good leg, blinked his one good eye in Emily Jane's direction and put one of his fingers from his one good hand in his one good ear and waggled it about.

'Ahoy there!' he said.

'You're looking, um, well, Poppycock,'

Emily Jane laughed.

Tripe coughed and spluttered a little and then hoisted up his trousers, which were forever slipping down. *'I've* not been too well of late, lass,' he commented.

'Oh, I'm sorry to hear that,' said Emily Jane.

Dave then smiled politely at Emily Jane and shook her by the hand. Being a Monkey Pirate just didn't seem to come naturally to Dave, who was very neat and very quiet.

Emily Jane knew things were about to happen. Just then Poppycock began to try

and juggle with the books from her bookcase. One-armed, one-legged, one-eared, one-eyed juggling rarely worked in Emily Jane's experience.

Poppycock's efforts were cheered on by the rest of the crew, who thought it was funny to see each book being thrown high into the air and landing all over the bedroom. Special cheers were given for books that bounced off other Monkey Pirates' heads.

Emily Jane didn't want to spoil anyone's fun, but she also knew that Monkey Pirates were excellent at adventures. If you saw adventures walking down the street, most of them would probably jump up and down a bit saying, 'Hello, I'm an adventure!'

Monkey Pirate adventures, on the other hand (especially when combined with Emily

Jane's imagination), would be the ones running down the street, doing cartwheels, bouncing off lampposts and shouting at the top of their voices, '**I'm an adventure, I'm an adventure!!!**' You just wait and see.

AAArrrgh!

IN WHICH A YOUNG GIRL'S IMAGINATION GOES ON A JOURNEY

Then the little girl went skipping down the lane, watched by a great big wolf that had teeth like garden shears and eyes like orange lights . . .

Hang on, that's another story. Sorry.

Emily Jane, being an adventurous little

girl herself, was very keen to set out on a new journey with the Monkey Pirates.

'Can we go somewhere then?' she asked. 'Can we find my Uncle Bartholomew?'

The Captain considered her request. 'You know what it will cost, don't ya?' he said.

Emily Jane did, and she reached under her bed and produced a bunch of bananas that she kept handy for such an occasion.

'Bananas and barnacles!' cried the Captain approvingly, as did the rest of the crew.

With that the twelve Monkey Pirates, plus

Emily Jane, clambered into the wardrobe again.

They were off on their adventures, which could take them anywhere in the world and to any place or time.

Although the wardrobe was cramped, Emily Jane's imagination found room to imagine where they might end up going. She imagined far-off countries with exotic names, cultures and smells. She imagined a land where the people wore strange hats and were all called Philip and sang songs about the sea,

like this one:

The sea is rather wet and blue,

And on the top float ships with their crew.

Down below where it gets much wetter,

Crabs and fish like it much better.

It's wobbly on the top and wobbly at the sides,

And it gets bigger and smaller according to the tides.

But when it stops the dryness begins,

The animals are less moist and don't have fins.

It should be mentioned at this point that Emily Jane's imagination comes with a warning and that warning is 'Please do not feed her imagination.'

AAAARRRRGH!

3

IN WHICH BERNARD BUMBOIL
HAS A SMALL ACCIDENT

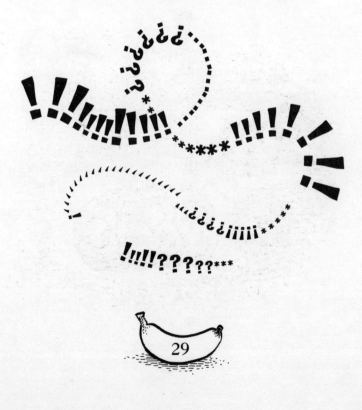

(NOW WASH YOUR HANDS.)

AAAAARRRRRGH!

IN WHICH A COURGETTE APPEARS IN A HANDKERCHIEF

Their first destination was frankly a bit disappointing after all of the twists and turns and general tomfoolery and shenanigans of Emily Jane's imagination.

They arrived in a very dull bedroom. They didn't know it, but it was the bedroom of a Mr

32

Graham Snape, the proud owner of a small greengrocer shop in the village of Linoleum-on-the-Naze, not far from Emily Jane's own house.

Graham Snape had been running the greengrocers all his life and he often said that fruit and veg were in his blood. Of course, nobody believed this until one day he produced a small courgette from his handkerchief after a particularly heavy nosebleed.

When the Monkey Pirates fell out of his

wardrobe, Graham Snape was busy in his shop and so he had no idea what had just happened.

The Captain took out his banana compass (a small piece of equipment with an arrow which identified the presence of all bananas in any direction – north, east, south or west). Then he sent the Monkey Pirates off to do what they do best.

And what Monkey Pirates do best, as you may have gathered, is create a little havoc and steal a lot of bananas. 'Bananas and barnacles!'

they shouted and disappeared from the room, leaving Emily Jane, the Captain and Dave.

Dave sat quietly reciting the Latin names for some flowers to himself, which left Emily Jane and the Captain together.

The Captain and Emily Jane sat and looked at each other. They exchanged glances. Emily Jane exchanged a slightly bemused glance for the Captain's sideways glance.

They exchanged thoughts and the Captain's one was, 'How is it that bananas always fit exactly into their skins?'

Emily Jane's thought was one that she had
had before and that was, 'Oh where, oh where
is my Uncle Bartholomew?'

And they exchanged addresses and while

Emily Jane's was complete with house number, street and post code, the Captain's merely read:

A wardrobe,

Space,

Time.

Emily Jane looked around her. 'Where are we exactly, Captain?' she asked.

'Well, where we are exactly, it be difficult to tell,' he began, 'but I tell you one thing. I reckon we're getting closer to where we want to be. The King of the Monkey Pirates has

always shown us the way and one day we will all travel together.'

'How do you know this?' asked Emily Jane.

'Aaaaarrgh! I just gets these feelings in me boots sometimes,' the Captain explained.

Emily Jane thought about this for a while and then took out her time-telescope and looked through it. There at the other end was her Uncle Bartholomew laughing and waving. (He was Emily Jane's most varnished and indeed vanished uncle and it was all a great mystery. It was a mystery greater than any

elephant's bottom,
and that was
saying something.)

Emily Jane
sighed heavily,
'Oh, Captain, do you think I will ever see my
Uncle Bartholomew again?'

The Captain smiled a strange smile and
said, 'Only time will tell, only time will tell.'
(He said this so that he sounded interesting
and wise and to cover up for the fact that he
didn't have a clue about her uncle.)

'Yes, perhaps you're right. I must say, that did sound interesting and wise,' said Emily Jane, and the Captain was pleased that he seemed to have got away with it.

Just then there was a lot of noise and cries of 'Bananas and barnacles!' as the rest of the crew burst through Graham Snape's bedroom door, all carrying bunches of bananas.

The Monkey Pirates ate the bananas and then squeezed themselves back into the wardrobe with Emily Jane.

'Right, let's go!' said the Captain and they

40

were off in a wardrobe bursting with banana-filled monkeys and a little girl.

'Oh, are we going then?' said Dave, who had nodded off for a while.

IN WHICH
THERE ARE NO BANANAS

Graham Snape's shop was very unlike the Monkey Pirates and was not in the least bit bursting with bananas. In fact, for the first time that he could remember, his shop did not have a full complement of fruit and veg and he couldn't find his bananas anywhere.

Graham Snape had always prided himself on being a first-class greengrocer and the lack of bananas began a slight panic in him. He laughed a nervous laugh.

Graham Snape's first banana-less day was not a happy one. It was made worse by the fact that he could have sworn he had seen some strangely dressed monkeys in his shop that afternoon. He didn't want that experience ever again so he decided to close his greengrocers the very next day and open something completely different.

After much consideration, he opened up a wardrobe shop called 'Wardrobes R Us'. This was just asking for trouble and, what's more, fruit and veg was still in his blood. (He cut himself on one of the wardrobes when he was filling the new shop and a small pea popped out.)

AAAAAAARRRRRRRGH!

6

IN WHICH A ROBOT APPEARS

This journey was much the same as all the journeys Emily Jane had had with the Monkey Pirates – very cramped with a strong smell of bananas.

What was unusual, however, was their arrival. Instead of tumbling out as the door sprung open, the doors hissed and slid

open smoothly, accompanied by a woman's voice that said, 'Please select your clothes preference by using the selection keypad.'

The Captain grabbed the keypad and all the Monkey Pirates tried to push the buttons. The contents of the wardrobe sprang out across the room, scattering clothes, shoes and hats everywhere.

'Aaaarrgh! Didn't fancy any of that lot anyways,' said the Captain.

Dave sighed slightly as a pair of shoes he rather liked the look of disappeared from view.

46

Emily Jane and the Monkey Pirates walked out into a white room with a large screen on the opposite wall.

'Look at all this. It's just like the things that I've read about in books,' said Emily Jane. 'This must be the future!'

'What is?' said Poppycock, squinting with his one good eye.

'This is!' said Emily Jane, gesturing at the room they were standing in.

'I don't gets it,' said a confused Poppycock.

Gobbledygook thought he would help and

looked very earnest as he said, 'Strup klimp grunp plot tet flampt spay.' He then crossed his arms and nodded in a very satisfied manner.

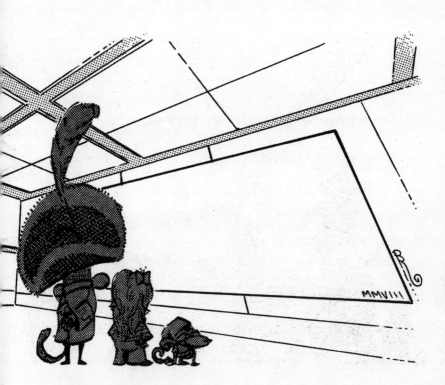

But Poppycock only looked even more
bewildered than before and just said,
'Errrrm!'

Perhaps Gobbledygook is not the best one

49

to explain the great mystery of time travel,
Emily Jane thought.

However, Gibberish did say, 'Aaaargh!
I gets it now' before losing his balance
and falling over. It was almost as if this
information had pushed something else out
of his brain. And that was exactly what had
happened. As there wasn't enough room for
all these thoughts in Gibberish's brain, he
had to lose something. This time it was
remembering how to stand up properly. He
then promptly forgot all about time travel and

got back to his feet.

'Aaaarrrgh, bananas and barnacles!' said the Captain, clearly unimpressed.

'It's all just gump-poot if you ask me,' swore Twaddle in agreement.

But before any more could be said on the subject, a door at the end of the room slid open and a robot whirled and hissed its way slowly towards them.

The robot was silver and shiny with a panel of lights that flashed and winked on its chest. Its arms were metallic tubes that extended

like telescopes and at the end there were metal fingers that opened and closed with little hissing sounds. The legs looked like pistons, and the whole thing glided across the floor as if it was ice-skating just above the ground.

It stopped in front of them. Emily Jane and the Monkey Pirates nervously waited for something to happen.

The robot's head turned slowly towards the girl and monkeys collected in front of it and its eyes flashed.

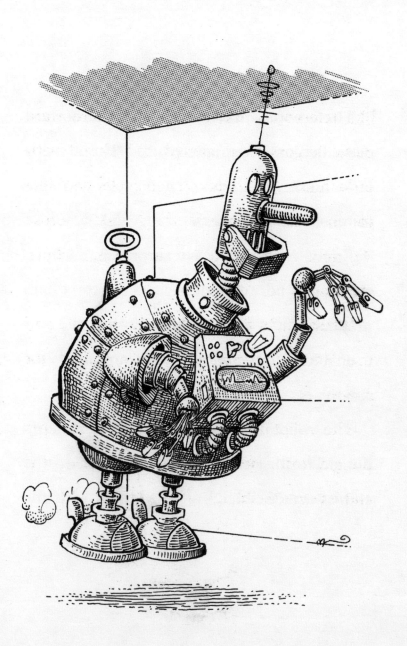

There was a pause. (Which could be best described as a dramatic pause.) There was a hiss and then . . . 'Ooooh, hello you! My name is Julian, what's yours?'

Emily Jane was a bit surprised, as most robots in her experience had letters and numbers for a name, like N174 or SP32 or even 0X22, but definitely not anything like Julian.

The Captain looked closely at Julian's domed head. He breathed heavily on to the shiny surface, wiped off the steam with the

sleeve of his jacket and looked at his reflection. He smiled at his image, adjusted his hat and winked at himself. *Now that be one handsome Monkey Pirate!* he thought to himself.

Then he took charge. 'I be Captain Banana S. Piranha and this be me crew.'

The Monkey Pirates called out their names:

'**Aarrgh! Piffle**,' said Piffle.

'**Aaarrrgh! Tripe**,' said Tripe.

'**Aaaarrrrgh! Balderdash**,' said Balderdash.

'**Aaaaarrrrrgh! Tosh**,' said Tosh.

'**Aaaaaarrrrrrgh! Gobbledygook**,' said Gobbledygook.

'**Aaaaaaarrrrrrrgh! Gibberish**,' said Gibberish.

'**Aaaaaaaarrrrrrrrgh! Drivel**,' said Drivel.

'**Aaaaaaaaaarrrrrrrrrgh! Twaddle**,' said Twaddle.

'**Aaaaaaaaaaarrrrrrrrrrgh! Guff**,' said Guff.

'**Aaaaaaaaaaarrrrrrrrrrrrgh! Poppycock**,' said Poppycock.

'And I'm Emily Jane,' said Emily Jane. 'I'm travelling through time and space in search of

my Uncle Bartholomew.'

'Er, excuse me, sorry, but I'm Dave,' said the final Monkey Pirate. 'I should have said my name a minute ago. Sorry.'

Dave still couldn't get the hang of being a pirate, despite his best efforts. He was questioning if he was really cut out for this sort of thing.

The rest of the Monkey Pirates, on the other hand, knew they were definitely cut out for this sort of thing. They loved bananas and they loved shouting, 'Bananas and

barnacles!' and they loved saying, 'Aaaarrgh!'

And so there they all stood, shouting, burping and scratching.

Julian considered the Monkey Pirates for a short while. 'Ooooh, how lovely!' he said. 'So, pirates on an adventure. I simply adore pirate adventures. And I love your boots!'

Some of the Monkey Pirates were giving each other strange looks and even stranger looks at the robot.

'Wangle splut klunk swank!' observed Gobbledygook.

Gibberish whistled and nodded in agreement.

'Anyway, as I said, my name is Julian,' said

Julian, 'and I'm a new design robot here to make sure you're comfortable. I specialise in soft furnishings and making tea.' With that, Julian produced a few cushions from between his legs, which made him look a bit like a large metal chicken laying eggs made of soft colourful material. He paused and then said, 'Well, who would like a nice cup of tea? You must all be parched!'

The Captain had thought that the robot was a bit odd before, but this offer of a cup of tea was too much. *Aaarrgh, he be dangerous,*

he thought, and then shouted, 'Bananas and barnacles!' before running out of the room, with the rest of his crew in hot pursuit.

Dave followed more slowly, thinking how lovely a mug of tea and a chat would be. But, not wanting to be left behind, he trotted after the others with Emily Jane.

'Sorry!' Emily Jane called back to Julian. Emily Jane knew she had to keep up with the Monkey Pirates as they were her only hope of finding Uncle Bartholomew, and her only way home.

'Well really!!' huffed Julian and turned himself off with a long hiss.

AAAAAAARRRRRRRRGH!

7

IN WHICH BALDERDASH
EXPLAINS HIS POINT OF VIEW

As they left the room the Captain checked his banana compass, which was going completely mad (madder than Balderdash when he discovers a fruit fly on his bananas).

'This be the way!' the Captain cried. 'There be real treasure here!'

The Monkey Pirates ran through white corridors and, every now and then, through sliding doors that hissed open in front of them saying, 'Please proceed' as they did so.

The Monkey Pirates just shouted, 'Bananas and barnacles!' at the doors.

Twaddle actually swore, saying things like 'Glob twang!' at each of the doors (but you probably don't need to know that).

Emily Jane was panting to

keep up and she apologised to each door as they had all been so very polite.

'Oh, I'm awfully sorry,' she panted.

'Beg your pardon,' she puffed.

'Excuse us,' she puffed and panted.

The Monkey Pirates were getting further and further away from her.

'Hey, wait for me!' shouted Emily Jane.

Monkey Pirates can move very quickly when they want to and quite obviously they wanted to at this moment in time.

Even Poppycock could move surprisingly quickly, given his overall leg count, and the short-sighted Drivel guided himself in the right direction by bouncing off the walls as he went.

Eventually, they came to a locked door and stopped and Emily Jane caught up with them.

'This be it!' said the Captain, pointing to the door.

As none of them were tall enough to see through the window that was set high up in the door, they decided to get on each other's shoulders.

Balderdash volunteered to be at the bottom of the pile (or rather, the other Monkey Pirates volunteered him to go at the bottom of the pile). They all climbed up.

'Ploock gump!' swore Twaddle. 'Careful with that thing,' he said and removed Poppycock's wooden leg from the top of his head.

67

Near the top was the Captain and on his shoulders sat Emily Jane. She pushed aside the feather that sprouted from his huge hat and peered through the window.

'Oh, my goodness!' exclaimed Emily Jane.

'What be it?' asked one of the Monkey Pirates.

'It's a banana and it's absolutely huge!' she said.

The Monkey Pirates became extremely excited and Balderdash tried to do a little jig. Then the entire monkey and girl pyramid

collapsed and they all crashed to the floor. Luckily, nobody was hurt, although Emily Jane vowed never to get on top of twelve monkeys ever again.

All this commotion came to the attention of a robot from inside the room. It opened the door and came out to investigate.

'You cannot enter. This is a restricted area,' the robot began saying, in that way that most robots tend to. All mechanical and not much fun. (And not in the least like Julian.)

'Fruit flies!' shouted the Captain.

Balderdash, who hated those creatures more than any of the other Monkey Pirates did, jumped. Monkey Pirates don't carry swords but they do carry whacking sticks that can be used to whack all manner of unpleasant things.

Balderdash cried, 'Dem bibbly shuck things. Cabbage-bum creatures. I 'ates dem!' as he always does when he hears the words 'fruit flies'. However, this time he also gave the robot several whacks, which sounded like banging a kettle with a cricket bat and made

a PHATUNG! noise.

The other Monkey Pirates took this

71

opportunity to stroll past the robot, leaving it with Balderdash to continue their conversation. It went a bit like this:

'This is a restricted area.'

'Dem cabbage-bum creatures!'

PHATUNG!

'This is a restricted area.'

'Dem cabbage-bum creatures!'

PHATUNG!

'This is a restricted area.'

'Dem cabbage-bum creatures!'

PHATUNG!

Meanwhile, the rest of the Monkey Pirates, along with Emily Jane, had walked into the room to find the huge banana. It was fat and flopped on its side, looking not unlike a giant yellow walrus sitting in a plastic case with tubes coming from it.

'It be enormous!' said the Captain and the Monkey Pirates all agreed it was by far the biggest banana that they had ever seen.

'Aaaarrgh! It's magnificent,' said Tripe and did a little cough to remind everyone that he was still not a well Monkey Pirate.

'Aaaarrgh! It's a beauty,' said Poppycock.

'Aaaaarrgh! Flam ling ploot tump krank,' said Gobbledygook.

'Aaaarrgh! Never seen anything like it,' noted Tosh.

'Aaaarrgh! It be fabulous,' said Gibberish, whistling in appreciation.

'Aaaarrgh! Tremendous – although it might be bad luck,' offered Piffle.

'Aaaarrgh! Wotpuck!' swore Twaddle in delight.

'Aaaarrgh!' went Drivel who, due to his

bad eyesight, had to take the word of all the others.

'Oh yes, it is quite large, isn't it?' observed Dave.

Around the room there were dials, bubbling test tubes, a machine that went 'ping' and many, many flashing lights. There was also another machine in the corner, which Tripe suddenly noticed.

'What be that?!!!!' he said and pointed to a small machine on a table. Everyone slowly turned with dread and foreboding

in the direction that Tripe was looking. (If there had been an orchestra there it would have gone dum, dum, DUM! But there wasn't and so it didn't.)

It was a machine about the size of a toaster and had been designed specifically to toast bread.

'Ummm, it's a toaster,' said Emily Jane.

'Oh,' said Tripe. 'Anyway, I've not been too well recently. Look at that,' he said, quickly pointing at something else instead.

In separate plastic cases, with tubes leading to and from them, were all manner of giant fruit and veg. There were tomatoes, pineapples, onions, pomegranates and radishes. Emily Jane and the Monkey Pirates couldn't believe their eyes.

It was Emily Jane who quickly realised what was happening. 'They are doing experiments to produce giant fruit and

77

vegetables,' she said.

'Yes, you're right,' said a man, who seemed to appear from nowhere but in fact had just come back from the toilet.

The man was big and friendly looking and wore a white laboratory coat. He had a large grey beard, probably the size of an English village plus an average sized badger added together.

'I've been expecting you, my friends, and I know what you want,' he said and laughed a deep, rolling laugh (one might even say

humphilated). 'I have produced all this giant fruit and veg and the banana is yours.'

'How did you know we were coming?' asked Emily Jane. 'Do I know you?'

'Oh, yes you do, young Emily Jane, but you know me as –' He suddenly stopped mid-sentence. 'What's that noise?' he asked.

They all listened.

'This is a restricted area.'

'Dem cabbage-bum creatures!'

PHATUNG!

'Oh, that be one of me crew in discussion

with one of your metal friends,' explained the Captain with a sigh.

'Anyway,' said the big kindly scientist, 'let me help you, but you must be quick.'

And with that the fantastically large-bearded scientist unplugged the tubes and opened the case containing the banana. 'Help yourselves!' he said.

The Monkey Pirates leapt on to the giant banana and between them they managed to haul the huge fruit out of its case and on to their shoulders.

81

The kindly scientist shouted out, 'Bananas and barnacles!' and as Emily Jane looked back he smiled and winked at her. He then disappeared out of sight (probably back to the toilet or to put some toast on or something).

The Monkey Pirates ran out of the room with the banana on their shoulders, followed by Emily Jane. Out in the corridor, Balderdash was still trying to explain his point of view to the robot.

'This is a restricted area,' said the robot.

'Dem cabbage-bum creatures!' insisted Balderdash.

PHATUNG! went Balderdash's whacking stick.

Balderdash caught sight of the huge banana the Monkey Pirates were hauling away. He took another look to be sure he had seen what he thought he had seen and, with a final

PHATUNG! he left the robot and ran after the rest of his crew.

The robot turned to watch Balderdash disappear down the corridor and said, 'Dem cabbage-bum creatures!' But Balderdash was too far away to hear the robot's changed opinion.

When they got back to the room where the wardrobe was, Julian the robot was fluffing up some cushions. He saw the Monkey Pirates dash in and looked at the huge banana they had with them.

'Ooooh, what a lovely big fruit!' he exclaimed excitedly.

Then he remembered that he wasn't talking to them and with a loud hissing noise like escaping gas he disappeared out of the room.

Now, twelve monkeys and one girl in one wardrobe is cramped enough, but when you have a banana the size of a large yellow walrus standing on its end in there as well, it's almost impossible.

'Look what you're doing with that thing,' said Tosh.

'Clump poot!' swore Twaddle as Poppycock stood on his toe with his wooden leg.

'Careful of the treasure!' shouted the Captain.

Eventually, somehow, they all managed to get in the wardrobe and Emily Jane hoped that this journey would be quick, as her face was being pushed against a very large banana by a monkey's bottom.

She also hoped this journey would now take her to her uncle.

IN WHICH SOMETHING VERY STRANGE HAPPENS

Thankfully, the journey was quick but it also resulted in a very strange happening.

When you are involved in time travel you can be sure of one thing and that is from time to time you will meet yourself.

As sure as eggs are eggs, bananas are

bananas and barnacles are barnacles you will bump into yourself. It might be yourself from the past or it might be yourself from the future, but bump into yourself you will. This is exactly what happened to Emily Jane and the Monkey Pirates on this occasion, but it was very unfortunate that it happened to happen in the new shop of Mr Graham Snape.

Mr Graham Snape was preparing for the grand opening of his new wardrobe shop. He had a showroom completely filled with wardrobes.

'Well, this wardrobe shop is the best move I've ever made,' he said to himself.

'No strangely dressed monkeys are going to appear around here,' he reassured himself.

'I mean, they don't come out of wardrobes, do they?' he reasoned and laughed. Then he popped to the shops.

All in all then, this was not a good place for twenty-four monkeys, two small girls and a very large banana to suddenly appear.

Now, when time travel does result in meeting yourself, it is important always to

carry a bit of chalk and to have a good labelling system. The Captain knew this and was prepared when they tumbled out of a wardrobe in Mr Graham

Snape's showroom to be confronted by another Captain and another eleven Monkey Pirates from a different wardrobe.

When Emily Jane saw another Emily Jane she was beside herself with excitement.

'This is fascinating,' said the first Emily Jane to herself.

'Yes, this is fascinating,' said the other Emily Jane to herself.

So there stood one set of Monkey Pirates from the past or future facing another set of Monkey Pirates from a similar place. The Captains agreed that they would write numbers or letters on themselves and each of their crew in order to avoid an embarrassing mix-up.

'Aaaarrgh, you be 'A',' began one of the

captains and wrote 'R.U.B.A.' on a crew member.

'No, no, that ain't be right,' he said and wiped it off and started again.

Eventually, with a little help from the Emily Janes (counting and the alphabet not being the Monkey Pirates' strongest points), the two Captains managed to complete the task.

'What be that?' asked Piffle, pointing to the chalk mark on his chest.

'That's a letter,' replied Emily Jane.

'Aaaarrgh, letters be bad luck,' said Piffle.

'Aaaarrgh, numbers be bad luck,' said the other Piffle.

Then the two Piffles both turned around three times and tweaked their noses to rid themselves of the bad luck.

Now, a group of Monkey Pirates with letters on them could spell trouble but as Monkey Pirates can't spell it was just a bunch of letters – twelve letters, in fact. However, if they stood in the right order it did spell 'S.P.A.G.H.E.T.T.I. P.I.E.'

The numbers, on the other hand, made no

94

sense at all, no matter what order you looked at them.

The numbers chosen were as follows: 3, 1, 7, 21, 106, 74, 83, 92, 5, 62, 109 and, of course, everyone's favourite, 42.

However, the interesting thing about the numbers was that if you added some of them up and then took some of the others away and did a little multiplication with the ones left over and put some others in a kitchen drawer and forgot all about them, you came to the same number as Emily Jane's age (probably).

So anyway, there stood two sets of Monkey Pirates, one with numbers on them and the other with letters on them, so that was all right. As for the Emily Janes, luckily they were dressed very differently. (One Emily Jane was still in her dressing gown but the other seemed much more prepared and was fully dressed.)

The Emily Janes went to say hello to each other and they were both very impressed with their own politeness and their shiny smiles,

their blonde hair, eyes of blue and cheeks of

pink. (They were both very colourful girls!)

'Hello,' said Emily Jane to Emily Jane.

'Hello,' replied Emily Jane.

This was also a great opportunity for all the

Monkey Pirates to meet themselves and so they did.

The Poppycocks took it in turns to spin each other round on their wooden legs. They also thought it would be fun to try each other's false teeth.

'Well, Poppycock and Poppycock seem to be enjoying themselves,' said Emily Jane.

'Yes, they do, don't they?' agreed the other Emily Jane.

The Tripes went off to describe their most recent illnesses and their symptoms.

'Aaaargh! I gets this pain all down me right side,' said Tripe.

'Me too, although it's affecting me left side as well,' said the other Tripe, not wishing to be outdone.

'Well, the other day I had a shooting pain that went straight down one side, up the other side, across the room and out of the window,' said the first Tripe. He then coughed a little.

The other Tripe coughed too, but added a sneeze and pulled up his trousers a bit.

They had never been happier.

99

The Twaddles swore at each other.

'Spoot clump! You even talks like me,' said one.

'Flump poot! You're right,' said the other.

The Piffles thought that having more than one Piffle was bad luck.

'Aaaaarrgh, you looks like bad luck to me,' said one Piffle.

'Aaaaaargh, so does you!' said the second Piffle.

The Guffs had a burping contest. They eventually had to declare a draw.

The Drivels walked past each other and ended up in a conversation with some furniture.

Gobbledygook chatted to himself. 'Fling

troop strang krup plimp,' said one.

'Clack woop prang blot,' said the other.

'Poop poop perchaders!' they both said together.

'It's good to see that Gobbledygook has someone else who understands what he is saying,' said one Emily Jane and the other nodded.

In fact, it was the first time ever each Gobbledygook could talk without Gibberish having to translate.

The Gibberishes were therefore at a loose

end so they relaxed and picked their noses and had a whistling contest.

Tosh stood next to himself, with two fleas called Pete standing on each of them.

'Oh, look over there, Pete,' said Pete.

'Oh yes, Pete,' said another Pete.

'That one looks just like you, Pete,' said yet another Pete.

'Yes, I suppose he does a bit, Pete,' said the final Pete.

The Captains told stories about themselves to each other. Stories of great braveness and

adventure during their many travels. Stories of treasure and triumphs over terrible monsters. Triumphs over monsters such as the Octa-snotty-pus – a slime of a creature with eight noses, a permanent cold and no

handkerchief. The Flabbyfartphant, which was a blast of an animal with a very big bottom and who lived on a diet of beans. And the Irkeasel, which was a cross between something rather irksome and a weasel. All defeated thanks to the bravery of the Captains!

The Monkey Pirates were having a great time.

This left the Daves together, who thought that they should practise their 'Aaaarrghs!' and try to become better pirates.

'Ummm, aaarrgh?' went one.

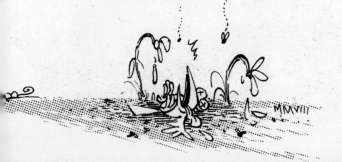

'Errrrr, aaarrgh?' went the other.

'Not too sure that was quite right,' said the first Dave.

'Perhaps a little louder?' suggested the second.

'I think so,' said Dave.

'Aaaarrgh!' they both went.

They looked at each other for a moment and then shrugged their shoulders.

'Fancy a bit of a read?' asked Dave and the other one nodded.

With that, the two Daves disappeared to

read some books about gardening.

Now, the Balderdash that had been labelled with a letter was very confused and so was the Balderdash that had been labelled with a number. Balderdash looked at himself and they both said, 'Bananas and barnacles?' and then 'Cabbage-bum creatures!' which started a fight.

The Emily Janes thought that it was a very strange sight to see two identical Balderdashes rolling around the floor arguing over identical

things. But it was quite funny too.

The only thing that brought an end to the battling Balderdashes was the huge banana being pulled into the middle of the room and peeled. This made all the monkeys sit down to feast.

It was at this point that Graham Snape arrived back to check on his stock of wardrobes. This is what is known as 'bad timing'. When he saw the monkey and banana-filled scene in front of him he decided to go and have a lie down on the sofa. He laughed a

strange little laugh. He must have been working too hard. He was going mad and seeing monkeys everywhere!

AAAAAAAAAARRRRRRRRRGH!

IN WHICH EMILY JANE BEGINS TO UNDERSTAND

The Emily Janes decided to take the opportunity to chat. They thought they would first check that they were the genuine article by asking each other a question.

'How many beans make five?' asked one.

'Um, a bean, a half bean, a bean and a half

plus two beans,' said the other (which was, of course, the correct answer).

They then took out their notebooks from their pockets.

'I've just started compiling "A Fairly Useful Guide to the Monkey Pirates",' said Emily Jane.

'Oh, I've written a few entries already,' said the other Emily Jane.

They swapped books to compare notes and when they returned them to each other they hurriedly scribbled some more notes.

'And have you found Uncle Bartholomew

yet?' asked one Emily Jane.

'No, have you?' replied Emily Jane.

'I'm not too sure,' said the other Emily Jane.

'Hang on, I've got an idea!' they both said together.

The Emily Janes then did something, the result of which nobody could guess. They placed their time-telescopes end to end and then looked through the lenses to see what would happen.

Time oozed together like wet sand from an egg timer squeezing between your toes. The

telescopes fizzed and crackled and images began to appear and both the Emily Janes saw the same thing. Pictures of men with various sized beards.

'Who's that with the small beard?' asked one Emily Jane.

'It's a man called the Professor, the inventor

of the wardrobe,' answered the other one.

'And who's that with the average-sized beard?' said the second Emily Jane.

'Oh, that's the kindly scientist,' answered the first.

Then they saw someone they both recognised. 'Uncle Bartholomew!' they cried in unison. 'What a huge varnished beard he has,' they agreed.

'Aaaarrgh, big varnished beards, you say. Sounds like the King of the Monkey Pirates to me,' said one of the Captains, who suddenly

appeared from nowhere and then disappeared just as quickly as he had appeared.

It was at that point that Emily Jane (both of them, in fact) realised a couple of things:

1. That it was true that two heads are better than one when it comes to these sorts of things, and

2. All these bearded men were in fact one and the same – Uncle Bartholomew!

'Bless my cotton socks!' said Emily Jane.

'Bless my cotton socks!' agreed the other Emily Jane.

The time-telescopes then had trouble coping with the whole situation. They gave off a little puff of steam, popped like a bubble in a large pan of stew and collapsed into several pieces.

Both Emily Janes looked at their time-telescopes and said, 'Oh dear!'

They collected together the pieces and placed them back in their pockets.

At this point Mr Graham Snape returned to the room. He saw that there were still strangely dressed monkeys in front of him. 'Monkeys,

monkeys, monkeys,' he cried in horror.

He decided there and then to close his wardrobe shop and try his hand at something nice and safe, like a beard care shop called Beards U Like. *Can't be any harm in that*, he thought.

And across space and time the Professor, the kindly scientist and Uncle Bartholomew stroked their beards thoughtfully.

After the two sets of Monkey Pirates had finished off the gigantic banana, they decided to go their separate ways.

There was much whooping and howling and many shouts of 'Bananas and barnacles!' and eventually they all got into their wardrobes.

There was a pause and one door opened and one Balderdash was flung out. The same happened from the other wardrobe. 'Flootscram! Get back to where you

118

should be,' said
Twaddle in
a rather
sweary
sort of way.

'Aaaarrgh!
Framp goot! You
ain't supposed to be
here neither,' swore the other Twaddle.

'Aaaaargh! A wrong Balderdash in your wardrobe can only lead to bad luck,' said Piffle.

'Aaaaarrgh! Mixing up your Balderdashes is just asking for trouble,' noted the other Piffle from the other wardrobe.

The two Balderdashes crossed the room, stopped, argued between themselves, got into a fight, slipped several times on the massive banana skin left on the floor and then went back to the wrong wardrobes. They got thrown out again, did the same thing twice more and then eventually ended up where they should be.

And so Emily Jane and the Monkey Pirates

(that is, the ones that spelt S.P.A.G.H.E.T.T.I.
P.I.E. when standing in the right order) went
off again and this time they ended up back in
Emily Jane's bedroom.

AAAAAAAAAAARRRRRRRRRRRGH!

10

IN WHICH
EMILY JANE HAS A VISITOR

Emily Jane's adventure felt like she had been away for several days (of course she hadn't, but time is like that sometimes).

She felt disappointed that the journey was over, but now she knew something very interesting. Uncle Bartholomew had indeed

vanished, but only to travel through time. He had different names at different times (and different sized beards, which got bigger as time passed). He was the Professor, the King of the Monkey Pirates and the kindly scientist and, most importantly, he was definitely her uncle. Also, Uncle Bartholomew had invented all the things that they said he had, wardrobes and time travel amongst them!

The Monkey Pirates shouted, 'Bananas and barnacles!' and disappeared and Emily Jane was by herself.

123

She put her hand into her pocket and pulled out the pieces of the time-telescope. She sighed sadly and placed them in a drawer.

Taking the notebook from her other pocket, Emily Jane flicked through the pages, smiling to herself as she re-read some of her notes. The Monkey Pirates certainly had fantastic adventures!

She considered the things that had

124

happened to her and began to wonder what it all meant.

Although Emily Jane had come closer to finding her uncle, he still wasn't back home with her. 'Will I ever see him again?' she thought to herself.

Just then, Emily Jane's mum called up the stairs, 'There's someone here to see you.'

Emily Jane went to the top of the stairs and looked down. There, standing just inside the door, was the large humphilating friendly figure of her Uncle Bartholomew!

He smiled a great big smile as friendly as a great big dog and as warm as toast.

Emily Jane shouted, 'Uncle, my uncle!' and ran down the stairs to him.

Uncle Bartholomew picked her up and swung her round, laughing. 'Have you missed me?' he asked.

'Well, I thought that I had but sometimes time plays tricks on you, doesn't it?' said Emily Jane.

Uncle Bartholomew just laughed again.

He does like a laugh, she thought.

Uncle Bartholomew and Emily
Jane went up to her bedroom
and they sat and
chatted for hours.
She learnt that
her uncle

discovered time travel one day when he had been varnishing his wardrobe and he'd passed on the secret to the Monkey Pirates. (A secret that they have always kept to themselves since they don't really understand how it works.)

'It was something I knew that the Monkey Pirates needed to keep safe,' Uncle Bartholomew explained. 'With the secret of time travel they could avoid Phileas Claxton,' he continued.

'Who?' asked Emily Jane.

'A man who wants to capture the Monkey Pirates for his circus in order to make his fortune,' said Uncle Bartholomew.

(Phileas Claxton is so rotten the less you know about him the better. Let's just hope he doesn't turn up in a later adventure.)

'Anyway, since then I have remained the friend of the Monkey Pirates and have become their King.'

'But why were you gone for so long?' asked Emily Jane.

'Oh, sorry about that,' said Uncle

Bartholomew. 'I forgot to take a watch and lost track of time.'

Emily Jane listened intently to her uncle's stories and told him about her adventures with the Monkey Pirates. 'They are so funny, aren't they, Uncle B?' she said.

'They certainly are. Now,' he said, changing the subject, 'as I'm here, let me fix that telescope of yours.'

Emily Jane took the parts from the drawer and handed them to her uncle, who took out a small screwdriver and some other tools and

quietly busied himself with fixing it.

'There!' he said in his big booming voice, which made Emily Jane jump, and he passed her the repaired time-telescope.

She looked through it to see an image of herself, Uncle Bartholomew and the Monkey Pirates all together.

'So, have you found your treasure?' asked Uncle Bartholomew.

'I think I have,' said Emily Jane. 'But does this mean it all comes to an end now?'

'Aaaaarrrgh! Bananas and barnacles! Only

time will tell,' he said and laughed. 'Anyway, I must be going. I noticed a beard care shop nearby – I thought I would give it a visit.'

Emily Jane gave her uncle a great big kiss on his cheek, avoiding the varnish on his beard. She watched him ambling up her street like a big bear until he disappeared from view.

She sighed. She was pleased to have her uncle back but would she ever see the Monkey Pirates again now? Would she ever travel with them again?

She didn't know the answers but she hoped

there were more adventures to come. She had a feeling that there would be Monkey Pirates tumbling out of a wardrobe near her soon.

AAAAAAAAAAAArrrrrrrrrrrrgh!

11

IN WHICH ONE STORY ENDS
AND ANOTHER ONE BEGINS

With stories about time it's often difficult to know where things finish and other things start.

This story is no different, and only time will tell if this is actually just the beginning of the story about Emily Jane and the

Monkey Pirates.

However, one thing we have learnt is that time waits for nobody, bananas wait for no monkey and Bernard Bumboil sometimes just can't wait!

A FAIRLY USEFUL GUIDE TO SOME MONKEY PIRATES (PART 2)

Your very own guide to keep, offering an essential quick reference to a number of the Monkey Pirates. This guide should be kept handy in case you meet one or more of the Monkey Pirates and will build into a complete works.

NAME: Tosh

RANK: A Bouncer of a Banana Buccaneer

DISTINGUISHING FEATURES: A happy home to two fleas, both of which are called Pete

LIKES: Scratching and not washing

INTERESTS: Shenanigans and banana juggling

FAVOURITE BAND: The Big Bearded Badger Sound

WISDOM: If it's straight and it ain't yellow then it ain't be a banana

WIT: What's yellow and invisible? No bananas

MONKEY PIRATE POINTS: 4.5 (out of 5)

137

NAME: Tripe

RANK: A Sneezer of a Banana Buccaneer

DISTINGUISHING FEATURES: An unwell Monkey Pirate, suffering from coughs, snuffles, sneezes and loose trousers

LIKES: Bananas, ointments, lotions and other medicines

AMBITION: To appear in a Hollywood film

HOBBIES: Shouting 'Bananas and barnacles!'

FEAR: Being teased by an overgrown leprechaun

MONKEY PIRATE POINTS: 4 (out of 5) ᘓᘓᘓᘓ

NAME: Twaddle

RANK: A Mug Whack of a Monkey Pirate

DISTINGUISHING FEATURES: Likes a bit of a swear

FAVOURITE SAYINGS: Swear words such as 'Sput Clack!' 'Crocklump!' 'Wotpuck!' 'Swattle' and 'Mug Whack!'

LIKES: Creating a brouhaha

FEAR: String

FAVOURITE DOUBLE ACT: Lulu Spangles and Derek Dogditch (The Dogditch and Spangles Experience)

MONKEY PIRATE POINTS: 4 (out of 5) ◟◟◟◟

NAME: Drivel

RANK: A Squinter of a Monkey Pirate

DISTINGUISHING FEATURES:
Can't see a banana in front of his face (but can always smell them)

FAVOURITE SAYINGS: 'Aaaarrgh! Bananas and barnacles!' to things such as hat stands, wardrobes, bookshelves and other things he mistakes as people on account of his poor eyesight

LIKES: Singing banana shanties

FEAR: Banana Trolls (if such a thing existed and we're pretty sure that they don't so it's not much of a fear really)

HOBBIES: Having a laugh

SECRET SKILL: He can whistle colours

MONKEY PIRATE POINTS: 4.5 (out of 5)

(Keep your eyes **peeled** for some more of this stuff.)

A FAIRLY USEFUL GUIDE TO THE AUTHOR AND THE ILLUSTRATOR

Your very own guide to keep, offering a quick reference to the people who wrote and illustrated this here book.

NAME: Mark Skelton

RANK: A Scribbler of Words

BORN: In a small house in Sussex with very little hair

CREW: 1 x wife (Amanda) and 1 x daughter (Emily)

RANK OF CREW: Both smashers!!

EDUCATION: Went to school with hair, went on to college with hair and then went to do a degree in Birmingham with lots of hair

WORK BACKGROUND: First job as a civil servant working in a Job Centre with slightly less hair and then worked in magazine publishing with even less hair

CONCLUSION: Work isn't good for your hair!!!

LIKES: All pleasant children and biscuits

DISLIKES: Rice-pudding

AMBITION: To buy a wig

NAME: Ben Redlich

RANK: Ink Lackey

BORN: At a very young age

NOW: Retired to a sub-tropical paradise (but only when eyes are closed)

CREW: 1 × very patient wife-to-be

RANK OF CREW: Undisputed Overlord

EDUCATION: Studied Animation for 3 years (didn't get certificates, but did leave with something much better [see 'Crew'])

WORK BACKGROUND: Cleaner of churches, filler of shelves, sewer of sock monkeys, and philatelist. Oh, and once worked two hours in a secondhand bookshop

LIKES: Fritters with spaghetti and mash

DISLIKES: Raw tomato

AMBITION: To breed exotic chickens and live in a Grant Wood painting

ACKNOWLEDGEMENTS

If you look up at the sky you'll see how very small we really are,

Like ripples from a pebble in a pond, we don't go far.

But have a look around at your circle of family and friends,

That same ripple can go far and might never end.

Moral: If you are going to be a plopped pebble in life, make sure

you have a good plop (or something like that?).

To Amanda and Emily – I love you both very much!!!

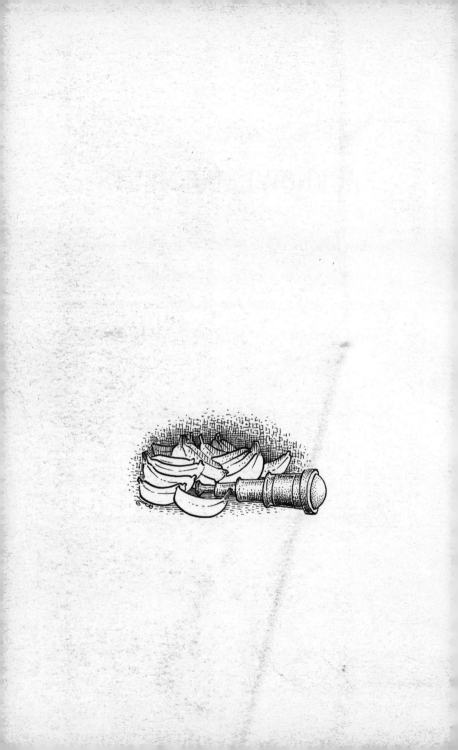